Toothy's Trouble

Thanks Crosby!
Enjoy the book!
♡ Mrs. B

Michele Barringer

Happy reading!
Michele Barringer

PAGE PUBLISHING, INC.
Conneaut Lake, PA

First originally published by Page Publishing 2021

ISBN 978-1-6624-2595-0 (pbk)
ISBN 978-1-6624-2596-7 (digital)

Printed in the United States of America

One night, twilight begins,
During quite a busy week,
She wakes, flutters, flaps, and spins,
Too groggy to make a peep.

Last night, she went to bed
With just a tiny sniffle.
A cold that filled her head,
Meant she slept but just a little.

She gathers up her things
In the fading light of day.
Solemn now, not at play,
But usually she sings.

Coins filling her satchel full,
She will leave each little child,
Closing her curtains with a pull,
The fairy flies through air so mild.

Her magic helps her visit
Each and every house.
She enters and leaves
As quiet as a mouse.

In the early light of sunrise,
She finishes up her work.
She has left a little surprise,
For the children, a little perk.

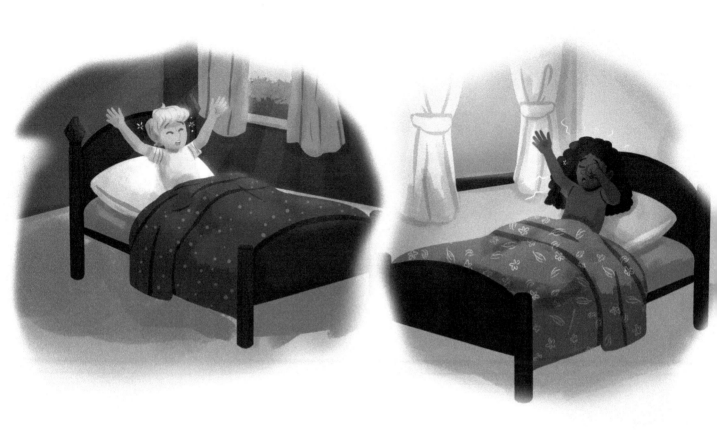

Flitting away in the golden rays of dawn,
The fairy makes her way back home.
She flies and stifles a giant yawn,
Ready for rest, weary from her roam.

Around the world as the day begins,
Children stretch and wake.
Smelling breakfast in their kitchens,
They find the prizes for the tooth she did take.

One by one, they open their hands,
Eager looks change to surprise.
The fairy altered all their plans
For the trinkets they'd buy with their prize.

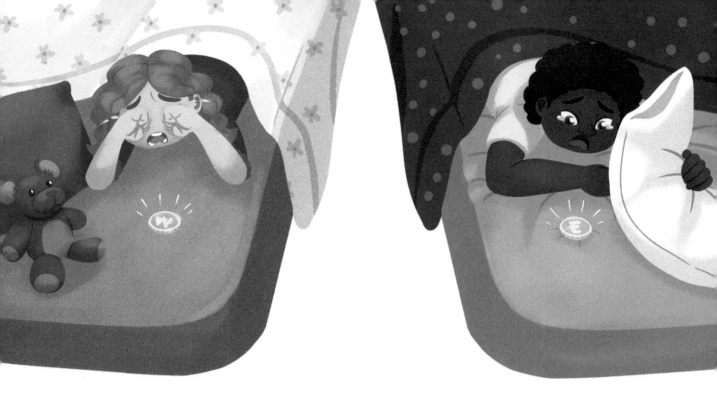

For Molly Mae in Sacramento,
She finds a peso instead of a dollar.
How will she buy that special memento?
Poor Molly Mae wanted to holler!

Francois in Paris was also upset.
A drachma was under his pillow.
Wanting a new toy, his eyes got wet,
And he cried to his sister Willow!

In Moscow, Little Anna anxiously looked,
And a lira was what she found.
She was saving for a brand new book,
But her smile became a frown.

In Buenos Aires, Pablo's found money,
Was a looney from Canada-Ay?
While at first, he found it quite funny,
All he couldn't buy here—hey!

On and on around the earth,
Children awoke to the same.
Getting strange money didn't cause mirth.
They wondered at the fairy's game.

In fairyland, dear Toothy slept.
She tossed and turned all day.
Awaking with a start, she leapt,
Feeling full of the dismay.

For poor Toothy felt the tears
Of each and every child.
Her strange dreams became her fears
Of her real mix-up oh so wild.

Quickly rising and getting ready,
She took a breath and made a plan.
Grabbing her bag, she got herself steady
And flew out into the night again.

The fairy flew as fast as she could
But realized she was running out of time.
If she could reverse the night, she would,
Because the eastern pink horizon was a bad sign.

As she arrived at the first child's room,
She couldn't believe her eyes.
Instead of tears, a smile in sleep.
What a great surprise!

As Toothy looked around the room,
She noticed lots of books.
Some maps, and lots of information
About the country's coin she took.

While at first, children were mad
But then grew eager to learn
About the new coins they had
And the new places and new terms.

It turns out that the children's learning grew,
Something new instead,
That was as good as holding something new,
They thought inside their heads.

As Toothy made her way back home,
With a smile upon her face,
She snuggled down in bed all prone,
Now in a peaceful place.

For Toothy's gigantic problem
Had turned out to be a treat.
A new interest had been found in them,
It was such a relief.

She would certainly be more full of care
When she now visited each kid.
Unless for fun, did she dare?
And switch up what she hid.

About the Author

Michele Barringer is a Western New York native who has been teaching in Michigan for twenty-three years. Teaching elementary children to love reading and literature over the years has been the highlight of her career, and she is now excited to share her own writing with readers of all ages.

When not working with students, Michele can be found reading novels, enjoying the garden, and spending time with her family and cats. Time at the lake is a favorite vacation for Michele with her husband and two children.